A Christmas Cannibal

Graveside Reads Vol 1, Issue 3

C.M. Saunders

Undertaker Books

Second edition 2025

Contents

I

Dylan Decker pulled the rim of his well-worn Stetson down over his eyes and shivered against the cold, his freezing fingers holding on to Skydance's reins. The afternoon was frigid and still, and the chance of snow hung in the air like a threat. It seemed like he had been on the trail for days. Actually, he *had* been on the trail for days. Three of them, to be exact, sleeping rough and drinking out of streams. Even hunting was out of the question in this weather. Other than a frozen possum he'd stumbled across, he'd been living on beans and jerky, and now his supply was dwindling. The only thing he craved more than a hot meal was a hot bath.

Dylan pulled on the reigns and slowed to a stop, then carefully dismounted to give Skydance a little break and stretch his own aching muscles. His buttocks were numb, and lately his legs had started cramping. He looked around at the featureless landscape.

At this time of year, the shadow of Christmas was everywhere. Everywhere there were people, anyway. He had come to dislike the festive season with a passion. It was all so corny and fake, and completely geared toward persuading people to spend money they didn't have on things they didn't need. Besides, you shouldn't require an excuse to be good to the people you were close to. Love was a gift that should be celebrated all year 'round, not once a year.

It hadn't always been this way. As a kid back in Pennsylvania, where he'd lived with his mother, father, and sister, he'd loved Christmas as much as anyone. Then, it was all about the gifts, candy, and fancy food. He remembered being given a leatherbound set of Jules Verne books when he was twelve. At that age he wasn't dumb enough to still believe in Santa Claus, and knew how much his parents had scrimped and saved to afford them. Those books had taken pride of place on a shelf at the family home ever since.

The novelty wears off when you grow up. The excitement ebbs away to be replaced with cold dissatisfaction and a vague sense of resentment. For better or worse, this time of year had a way of making you get reflective and take stock of your life.

It was usually for the worse.

This year he would be happy with a warm bed for the night, but even that seemed to be out of his reach. He hadn't seen another human for days, let alone a town of any description. The sun would be setting in a few hours, and if he didn't find civilization by then he was going to have to make camp for the night. It wasn't ideal. Being a wayfarer during the winter months definitely wasn't for everybody. But it wouldn't be the first winter night he'd spent outdoors.

As much as he tried to tell himself it was just another day, he was powerless to prevent intrusive thoughts of Christmases past from running through his mind. All things considered, it was a mixed bag. Those warm, fuzzy, innocent childhood memories rubbed shoulders with darker, more insidious recollections, some of which he carried like physical scars. The solitude, the loneliness, the search for redemption in the bottom of a whiskey glass.

Perhaps the best thing about Christmas was it made most people he met on his travels friendlier and more cheerful than they were under normal circumstances. It was almost as if for one day a year, everybody put aside their differences and made the extra effort to get along.

Now that he thought about it, wasn't that also fake? People who wouldn't piss on you if you were on fire any other time now wanted to be your friend just because it fit the narrative and made them feel better about themselves.

It was a damned shame that whatever instinct forced people to act that way couldn't be made into an elixir and sold by the bottle. Then again, who would buy it? It wouldn't be much use unless everybody drank it.

Charlie Robbins suddenly barged into his mind, all goofy smiles, tall stories, and shoulder-length blond hair. In another life he could have been a famous stage actor. God, how long ago had it been? Three years? Could it really be that long? Dylan remembered everything as if it had happened only yesterday.

II

DYLAN WAS PASSING THROUGH the heart of Texas. There was a snowstorm, a blue norther blown down from the plains, and he was doing his best to push through it, which was becoming increasingly difficult as the snow obscured the trail he was on. It was dangerously close to a white-out, and he had slipped into a kind of fugue state where the only thing that mattered was putting one foot in front of the other. Or more accurately, making sure Skydance put one foot in front of the other. In conditions like that, it's easy to walk your horse off a ledge or straight into a freezing river.

Suddenly, away to his right, he spotted a flickering light. At first, he thought he must be imagining it. Then he was filled with a fleeting fear that he might be seeing a ghost or a siren trying to tempt him off the path to his doom. He'd heard stories of such things before. But when he looked closely, he saw the light for what it was. A fire.

Hesitantly, he steered Skydance toward the warm glow.

As Dylan approached, through the swirls of snow he saw someone had tied a tarp between two chest-high tree stumps and used a huge boulder to provide a back wall to the makeshift camp. Stretched out next to the boulder was a beautiful sleek white Arabian steed.

The fire was under cover, and it took a few seconds for Dylan's eyes to adjust and make out the huddled form of a man. He slowed warily, knowing that approaching a stranger's camp uninvited was a good way to get filled with holes.

A few yards away, the hunched figure shifted slightly. Dylan wiped moisture from his eyes as he tried in vain to see if the man was armed. He'd be more surprised if the stranger wasn't, and his right hand went to the butt of his Colt Peacemaker. Just in case.

The figure cocked his head in Dylan's direction and raised a hand, making Dylan's heart stop momentarily. Was he signalling to him or someone else? Then the hand waved, and a man's voice yelled, "Come on in, partner! Weather out there's lousy!"

Dylan paused long enough to look around to make sure he wasn't about to be blindsided. He couldn't see more than ten feet in any direction, but old habits die hard. When he saw he wasn't under imminent attack, he proceeded toward the camp, dismounted, and tied Skydance up next to the boulder. There was no room in the camp for him, but at least here he'd get some heat from the fire. He'd probably be happy to just rest. With two horses and two men in such close proximity it would be a tight squeeze, but the body heat would help them all survive this hellish night.

With Skydance settled and stripped of saddlebags, Dylan draped a blanket over the horse's back and finally turned to greet his new acquaintance. Wrapped in a woollen shawl and face partially obscured by a Stetson, the stranger motioned for Dylan to sit next to him by the fire and held out a hand to be shook. It was cold.

"Thank you kindly, friend," Dylan said by way of greeting.

"Think nothing of it," the stranger drawled. The bottom half of his face broke into a wide, toothy smile, and Dylan took note of the curls of fine blond hair protruding from under his hat and resting on his shoulders. He had never seen hair like that on a man before, but imagined that on nights like this it was a great benefit.

"Name's Charlie," the stranger continued. "Charlie Robbins."

"Nice to meet you, Charlie," Dylan said, manoeuvring a slightly concave boulder closer to the fire and letting out a sigh of relief as he lowered his bulky frame onto it. "Makes a refreshing change to meet someone willing to help out a stranger."

"Well," Charlie Robbins began, "it's Christmas Eve, ain't it?"

After weeks on the trail, Dylan had lost track of the days, but he knew Charlie was right. . "In that case," he said, "It's the perfect time to polish this off."

Reaching over, he opened one of his saddlebags and pulled out a half-empty bottle of Old Fitzgerald bourbon.

"Wow," exclaimed Charlie. "Is that genuine Old Fitz?"

"It is indeed," Dylan replied, his chest swelling with pride. "The twelve-year-old kind. It's pretty hard to get. Picked this up on a steamship in Kentucky. About the only place you can get it. There and some of them fancy private members clubs. I been keeping it for a special occasion, and it looks as though this occasion is about as special as it's gonna get anytime soon."

Dylan took a deep swig and grimaced as the liquid burned a trail down his throat. Wiping his mouth with the back of his hand, he passed the bottle to his new friend. The kid seemed to be at least fifty percent teeth at the best of times, but that made him smile even harder. He wasn't technically a kid. Dylan had him pegged at about twenty-five, but had already reached the stage in life where everybody younger than him was a 'kid.'

"You headed to town?" Charlie asked.

"Didn't know there was a town near." Dylan shrugged. "I been making this up as I go along."

"Well, not every man needs a plan." Charlie shrugged back. "This place is called Wagnerville, five or six miles down the road, I guess. Famous for its sausages."

"Can't be that famous. I never heard of it."

"I'd be glad to introduce you!" Charlie said, grinning again. "They sell 'em in bread rolls with fancy sauce. Best in the state, they say."

"I could just about murder one of those right now," Dylan said as his empty stomach growled.

"Why stop at one? I'm fixing to put away at least four, then have a lie-down, and then four more!"

Both men laughed.

"Why didn't you push on and grab yerself a warm bed for the evening?" Dylan asked, curious.

"Weather got so bad I could barely see my hand in front of my face," Charlie explained. "Didn't wanna risk Buttermilk here turning his leg over."

"Fair enough," Dylan agreed. "Can't be taking chances with a horse like that."

"He's a beaut, isn't he?"

"He is."

Oftentimes when you met strangers on the road, conversation was stilted or awkward. You were both on the defensive, and only talked when you had no other choice. This meeting felt different. Charlie Robbins seemed a likeable sort. He had that charm, and still held on to that youthful enthusiasm you often see in men before life beat it out of them. It reminded Dylan what it was like to be that age. Strong and fearless, and filled with a sense that the whole world revolved around you.

It turned out they had a lot in common. Both came from coal mining families and had British roots. Dylan's ancestors coming from Wales, and Charlie's from Scotland. They were also in the same kind of business, which was any business, scraping a living any way they could.

They traded stories next to the fire and drank bourbon until it ran out. Then Dylan retrieved a pack of cigarettes and shared those as well. He was glad he had them instead of rolling tobacco because though it was a lot warmer in camp than out, his fingers were still too cold to roll.

Within a couple of hours, with their supplies exhausted, the men decided to turn in. Charlie heaped some wood he'd been drying on top of the fire to sustain it as far into the night as possible while Dylan cleared a space to lay his sleeping bag. He went to sleep basking in the warm glow brought about by good company and just enough whiskey.

III

DYLAN WOKE UP SHIVERING. His eyelids fluttered open, and he quickly closed them again when a stabbing pain shot through his head. That was what drinking on an empty stomach did to you. Even if you drink the finest bourbon.

He opened his eyes again, more slowly this time, and was shocked at the sight that befell him. The tarp that provided shelter the night before was gone. Everything was gone. Still in his sleeping bag, Dylan sat up and looked around, rubbing his eyes as he struggled to process everything.

There was no sign of Charlie Robbins, nor Buttermilk, his white Arabian horse. The only hint that they had been here at all was the scorched remnants of the fire and the blackened ashes blowing around in the wind. Worse than that, Skydance was gone, along with Dylan's winter coat, Winchester rifle, and saddlebags, which contained just about everything he owned.

He'd been robbed.

That scheming, two-faced turd Robbins had cleaned him out.

He pounded a fist into the thawed earth next to him and let out an anguished scream. How could he be so stupid? So much for the Christmas spirit. He'd known that kid had been too damn nice.

Still raging, Dylan rolled up his sleeping bag and looked around despairingly as he assessed his options. The way he saw it, he didn't have that many. At some point during the night it had stopped snowing, but not before it had covered any tracks Charlie Robbins may have left. The fresh, powdery snow was now a few inches deep, maybe a couple of feet where it had drifted. Dylan could freeze to death out here. At least he had fallen asleep with his boots on, or the little asshole would probably have made off with those too, and that would have been a death sentence. He was also still in possession of his Peacemaker and Bowie knife, which he used to cut open one side of his sleeping bag so he could fashion some kind of garment to keep out the worst of the chill. It might buy him some time.

He had to get moving.

But where?

The robbing toad had said something about a town a few miles down the track. But what track? All he could see was virgin snow.

"Damn it!"

Dylan stomped his feet in frustration and looked around. It was deathly quiet. The wildlife had better sense than to venture out on such a frigid morning, and even the carrion birds had left for sunnier climes. Away to his right lay an impenetrable pine forest, which helped him get his bearings and gauge which way he should be facing. All he could do then was walk.

It was tough. Despite the sleeping bag draped over him he couldn't stop shivering, and his boots crunched in the snow as he trudged ever onward. As he couldn't tell whether he was on any kind of path or not, he hung his hopes on coming across a hunter's cabin or, failing that, some friendly stranger who could help him out of this mess. He chuckled to himself, remembering what the last "friendly stranger" he met had done.

At times, he didn't just walk, he marched, always careful to keep the pine forest on his right and then behind him to maintain a straight(ish) line. He didn't know where he was going, but knew he was going somewhere and that had to be enough. Often, he muttered to himself, other times he broke into song. Christmas carols worked well. He appreciated the irony. All that stuff about merriment and good will to all men. But most of the time, he occupied himself with bloodthirsty fantasies about what he was going to do to Charlie Robbins when he finally caught up with him.

It started snowing again, and the wind kicked up the fresh powder that had already fallen. Time lost all meaning. He was out of breath, and every step he took sent a searing pain through his calves. He wanted nothing more than to stop and rest. But he knew if he did that, it would be the end of him. Someone would find him frozen solid days or weeks from now. That was assuming the animals didn't tear him apart and scatter his bones.

All the while he felt the weight of his Peacemaker bumping against his hip, and in his darkest moments he thought about turning it on himself. A loud bang and a flash of light and it would all be over. It must be a better end than slowly freezing to death. What did he have to live for, anyway? Life was pain. And not just the physical kind. The longer he lived, the more the regret piled up.

But he couldn't do it. Wouldn't. No matter how bad things got, wilfully checking out was not an option. He was far too stubborn for that.

And so he went on. And on. In place of the pine forest was now an open plain, and a jagged mountain range rose on his left. Some time later, he saw smoke rising in the distance. It was barely perceptible against the gray sky, but it was there.

As he squinted through the swirling snow, he began to make out straight lines against the landscape. There were no straight edges in nature. He must be looking at a building.

And the smoke meant there must be people.

With a renewed sense of purpose Dylan bowed his head against the brittle wind and increased his pace, pushing through the pain barrier for what seemed like the hundredth time that morning alone. By the time the town opened up in front of him, he was almost on all fours.

Wagnerville, the sign said.

The name was familiar, but Dylan didn't dwell on it. He was so relieved to find civilization that he was close to tears.

The town was small and compact, but vibrant and less run-down than most places he visited. Despite the abominable weather, it was thriving. The snow had been cleared from the street and shoveled into neat piles on the side of the road, allowing residents to go about their daily business. Next to the town's sign was an oversized Christmas tree, undoubtedly taken from the pine forest he had seen earlier. Far removed from its poor cousins, this pine tree had been lavishly decorated with brightly colored baubles and clumps of berries.

In among the usual establishments you'd expect to find on the main throughfare of any decent-sized town such as a bank, a post office, a saloon, a general store, a tailor and a butcher, Dylan noticed several more unique premises. On his left was a glassmaker, according to a sign hanging over the door. There was also a fancy delicatessen, and even a wine shop. Every window was adorned with colored orbs and strips of paper.

He decided to look for the sheriff's office. Someone there might be able to help him find Charlie Robbins, assuming that was his real name, and the name they knew him by, if they knew him at all. He could at least report

Skydance's theft and leave a description in case he turned up somewhere. It was a long shot, but stranger things had happened. It was a funny old world.

Then, he caught the scent of something on the breeze and suddenly found himself intoxicated. It was exotic and spicy, yet meaty and wholesome.

Hot food.

Stomach gurgling, Dylan sniffed at the air. The smell seemed to be coming from the other side of the street. He turned around to investigate, following his nose until he found the source: a gaudy red and white shopfront with an oversized painted sign featuring a giant, curved sausage with a fork stuck in it.

Beneath the sausage sign was a little serving hatch manned by a large, mustachioed man wearing an immaculate white apron. He eyed Dylan suspiciously through a pair of thin, wire-rimmed spectacles. His beefy, pale arms, folded in front of him like two slabs of meat, were completely hairless. Shaved.

And that was when Dylan first saw the sleek white Arabian tied to a hitching post outside.

Buttermilk?

Charlie Robbins was here.

IV

OF COURSE! WAGNERVILLE MUST be the German town with the famous sausages Charlie had been bumping his gums about.

But they could wait.

He had a score to settle.

Just as Dylan approached the store, a door next to the serving hatch opened and out walked Charlie Robbins himself, stuffing something into his mouth as he walked. Mustard was smeared on his chin.

"Hey you!" Dylan growled, shrugging off the sleeping bag that had been keeping him warm and hovering his right hand above his Peacemaker. "Where's my goddamn horse?"

Charlie Robbins froze mid-step. For a split second, his eyes widened with shock, then his face broke into that trademark grin of his. "Hey...man!"

"Decker! My name's Decker. Dylan Decker."

"Sure, of course I know that!" Charlie said. "Don't you worry about a thing, Decker, my man! Your horse is up in the stable on the edge of town getting fed, watered, and groomed. It was going to be my Christmas gift to you. Thought I could come down here early, get him fixed up, buy us some sausages, and make it back to camp before you woke up. I guess I lost track of time."

The kid was so convincing, Dylan almost believed him.

Almost.

"Lost track of time, huh?" Dylan could feel the rage bubbling and it was all he could do to prevent himself from surrendering to it. "You're a goddamned liar! You left me out there to die, probl'y thinking I wouldn't make it this far on foot."

There was another pause, and in that moment, Dylan knew he had hit the nail right on the head.

"That's...crazy talk," Charlie said, grinning again. Except now, it was more of a sneer and it had slipped slightly, as if he knew the jig was up. "If I wanted to kill you, I would have."

Dylan considered this for a moment, then dismissed it. All it did was prove the kid was a coward as well as a thief and a liar. Cutting a man's throat while he slept and sneaking off with all his stuff in the middle of the night were two completely different things.

"If you don't believe me, here's the ticket," Charlie said, thrusting a little piece of pink paper in Dylan's face. "You give that to the boys in the stable and they'll give you the horse. While you're doing that, I'll go back inside and get you a warm sausage in a bread roll with all the trimmings. You gotta try these things. I'm already on my third. Can you smell that meat?"

Dylan could indeed smell the meat, and it was making his mouth water. But first things first. He snatched the receipt out of Charlie's hand, picked up his sleeping bag, turned, and headed up the street. He hadn't passed any stable on the way in, so it must be at the other end of town.

Had he been thinking straight he might have forced Charlie to come with him at gunpoint, but that might cause problems in a civilized place like this. Besides, being angry was exhausting. All he could feel now was relief. He just wanted Skydance back.

The stable was right where he thought it would be. The stable hand took the receipt out of his hand, looked it over, and came back with Skydance. When the horse saw Dylan, he snorted and flicked his mane as if to seek approval. He had indeed been washed and groomed. Charlie hadn't been lying about that. But isn't that exactly what you would do before selling a horse?

His saddlebags were also at the stable, along with his winter coat and Winchester. Dylan took some time making sure all his things were still there. And they were. Presumably only because Charlie hadn't had time to move them on yet.

He decided to make his way back down to the sausage shop to teach the kid a lesson, providing he hadn't run off again. Dylan didn't know what he would do when he saw him. He might yell, pick him up and shake him, or just shoot him in the face. But he would find out soon enough.

Riding Skydance had never felt so good, and Dylan promised his horse he would stop at the general store when all this was over and stock up on treats. It was Christmas, after all. It might have been his imagination, or the grooming session, but he could have sworn Skydance also had an extra spring in his step.

Buttermilk was still hitched outside the sausage shop, but there was no sign of Charlie. Dylan dismounted, tied Skydance to the hitching post, and walked up to the serving hatch. The large, mustachioed man with the immaculate white apron and smooth arms looked up from his work.

"What can I get you?" he asked in a choppy European accent Dylan assumed was German.

He had every intention of seeking out Charlie Robbins, and only Charlie Robbins, but seeing as his horse was right here, he couldn't be far away.

And that smell!

Dylan felt as if someone was reaching inside him and twisting his innards around. "Not sure," he replied, trying to play it cool. "What're you selling?"

"Dachshund sausages."

"I thought that was a sort of dog."

"It is. The breed is also known as a sausage dog."

"So you make sausages out of dogs?"

"No," the man said, slapping aside Dylan's rudimentary attempt at humour. "They're made from pig. Mostly. We call them Dachshund sausages because of the shape. Long body, no? I can fix you one with bread, mustard, and sauerkraut."

"What's that?"

"Sauerkraut?" the man asked, seemingly surprised that Dylan didn't know what he was talking about. "Fermented cabbage. German delicacy."

"Doesn't sound like much of a delicacy to me. In fact, it sounds like the last thing I would want on my plate."

The man shrugged.

"Fine," Dylan said. "How much would that set me back?"

"Thirty-five cents."

Dylan thought about it. It wasn't cheap. If he spent thirty-five cents in a general store, he could probably get enough food for three or four meals. But it was Christmas.

"I'll take one," he said, wiping his hands on the front of his dirty shirt in anticipation.

The man in the white apron simply stared at Dylan, unmoved.

It took Dylan a few moments to work out what was happening. "Oh, I'll be right back."

He hurried back to Skydance and rummaged in the saddlebag until he found his purse. He counted out thirty-five cents, went back to the serving hatch, and placed the money on the counter. Then he watched, transfixed, as the man in the white apron used a pair of tongs to pluck a gigantic, curved, dark brown sausage from a vat of boiling oil or water, placed it in a white bread roll, spread mustard and a spoonful of white stringy vegetables on top, which Dylan guessed was the sauerkraut, wrapped the creation in a paper napkin, and handed it over.

"Pleasure doing business with you, too," Dylan muttered as he lifted the steaming bundle to his mouth. Then he stopped. There was just one thing that could make this moment better. A seat.

He pushed the door to the sausage shop open and stepped inside. Immediately, the warmth cocooned him like an embrace. The interior was spotless, the walls covered with posters and picture frames and the floorspace divided into booths. At the far end was a door. A storeroom, Dylan guessed.

The restaurant was deserted, and a large clock on a wall otherwise adorned with framed pictures gave a hint as to why. It was just after 3 p.m. Between lunch and dinner. Even in Germany. Probably.

Slumping into one of the booths, Dylan primed himself and finally took a huge bite out of one end of the sausage in its bread roll jacket and moaned aloud when his taste buds exploded into life. A soft thump came from somewhere nearby, which he immediately dismissed. This moment was too precious. Before he was even finished, he was already considering buying another one. Or even two. Charlie Robbins had been right: one just wasn't going to be enough. The fermented cabbage was simply glorious, and the meat was to die for.

"What do you think you're doing?"

The voice was deep and authoritative. Startled, Dylan turned to see the man with the white apron standing over him. From Dylan's seated position, the man appeared even more intimidating. His folded, hairless arms rippled with muscle.

"Excuse me?"

"I asked what you think you're doing."

"Well, I'm sitting here eating the sausage I just bought from you," Dylan replied, bewildered. "Which might just be the best thing I ever ate, by the way."

"Please leave."

Dylan was confused, and couldn't even be bothered to hide it. "Why? Are you shutting up shop?"

"No."

"Then can't I sit here for a while? You wouldn't believe the day I've had."

"No."

Dylan could tell this was going to be a challenge. He was no great conversationalist himself, but compared to this guy he was a poet laureate. "I'm not sure I understand."

"You don't need to. Just get out. Now."

Dylan knew enough about common law to realize that he had no choice but to acquiesce. It was this man's business, his premises, and his chair. If he didn't want Dylan sitting in it, it was up to him.

But Dylan wasn't going to go without a fight. "Jeez," he said. "Are all German folk as warm and friendly as you?"

"No."

Again, the attempted sarcasm went right over the man's head. In the midst of it all came that muffled thump came again. Twice in quick succession. Dylan thought he saw the shopkeeper's eyes dart toward the door in the back.

What the heck was going on here?

Nothing to do with him, that's what was going on here, Dylan scolded himself. Poking your nose into other people's affairs was an easy way to get hurt. Or worse.

He slowly crammed the last of the sausage in his mouth and wiped his chops with a napkin without taking his eyes off the big German. Damn, that sausage was good. But he wouldn't be spending any more of his hard-earned money in this joint. There was more to running a business than making good sausages.

"Guess I'll be on my way," he said, getting to his feet. Even at full height, his eyeline was just about level with the man's Adam's apple. If this guy said it was Tuesday morning, it was Tuesday morning. No sausage was worth this amount of trouble.

Dylan was turning to leave when he heard a muffled voice say, "Mister Decker? Is that you?"

V

DYLAN STOPPED.

"What was that?"

"What was what?" the big German replied, positioning himself between Dylan and the door at the back.

"I heard someone call my name."

"I didn't."

This was too weird. Nobody in this town even knew him. Except Charlie Robbins.

"Mind if take a look back there?" Dylan asked, nodding at the door.

"Yes," the man replied with a deadpan expression. "I mind."

Dylan hesitated, his senses on high alert. Something was wrong here. Very wrong. And he was going to find out what. It wasn't in his bones to let it lie.

Summoning up all his newfound energy, he exploded into action and shoved the big German as hard as he could. Caught by surprise, he stumbled backward and tripped over his own feet, buying Dylan a valuable few seconds.

He ran past the man on the floor and several empty booths, reached the door at the back, and turned the handle.

It was locked.

Taking a step back, he swung a hefty boot at it, making the door shudder in its frame.

From behind the door came a strange whine, and then: "Help me!"

Dylan kicked out again, this time with more force. The lock splintered, and the door flew open.

He wasn't ready for what he found in that little repurposed storeroom.

Boxes and crates were piled in the corners and stacked against the walls, but most of the space was taken up by a rickety wooden table. Spreadeagled and strapped to it was Charlie Robbins.

But he wasn't smiling anymore.

His eyes were sunken, his cheeks sallow, and his mouth agape. Around his neck was what looked like a ball gag which had worked loose.

As Dylan's gaze worked its way down Charlie's body, the terror began to build. He was wearing the same clothes he had been when Dylan last saw him not an hour earlier, and his arms, torso, and head appeared to be unharmed, apart from a large purple bruise on his forehead. But his lower body was a different matter.

His jeans had been cut away, shreds of denim hanging down over the sides of the table, and the flesh of his thighs was gone. It looked as if it had been neatly sliced away, rather than bitten off in chunks as you would expect from an animal attack, and buckets had been placed around the table to catch excess blood as it ran off. Through the terrible, gaping wounds, Dylan could see bones, some of which seemed to have been broken and splintered.

A sledgehammer was propped against the far wall next to a small nightstand, upon which lay a blood-stained meat cleaver, some other cutting tools, and a bowl.

Charlie's ruined body suddenly began to shudder as if he was convulsing, and white froth trickled from the corner of his mouth. When the tremors subsided, he turned to look at Dylan, who was still frozen in the doorway.

"H-Help me," he croaked.

Dylan didn't know what had happened here, and truth be told he didn't much care. He didn't believe in God, but he did believe that a man reaped what he sowed in life. Whatever this was, Charlie probably had it coming.

But before Dylan could turn on his heels and get out of there, something hit him from behind, propelling him forward. He inadvertently kicked one of the buckets of blood, sending the foul liquid cascading over the floorboards, and collided with the table, flipping it over and dumping Charlie, or what was left of him, onto the floor.

Before Dylan could process what was going on he felt himself being hoisted up by his belt and suspenders and thrown headfirst into the wall. He heard something crack, and hoped it was the plaster and not his skull. Then he landed in a heap with his arms up over his head, so disoriented that he didn't even know which way was up.

The first thing he saw when he opened his eyes was Charlie Robbins. He was still lashed to the table but now only by one wrist, and he was reaching out imploringly while his bottom half trailed uselessly behind him. Dylan planted his hands on the blood-soaked floor and tried to scoot away, only to find a wall behind him.

"They're eating me," Charlie whispered, eyes wide with horror. "Eating me!"

Then a huge shape loomed and all Dylan saw was a gigantic fist crashing toward the center of his face.

The impact made his nose explode with pain and sent the back of his head into the wall again. He tried to sit up, but there was not enough room to maneuver himself. It suddenly dawned on him how dire the situation had become. He could die here, in a sausage shop storeroom on Christmas Day, and nobody would ever know.

Making the most of the limited space, he allowed himself to topple onto his left side. In doing so, he narrowly avoided another punch and, more importantly, freed up his right hand. He reached for his Colt, drew, and pointed the revolver.

It was the big German guy with the mustache.

Who else?

Dylan didn't care what his deal was. He had crossed the line, and now he was going to pay.

Dylan thumbed back the hammer, delighting at the shiver of anticipation that went through him when it clicked into place. But before he could pull the trigger, the German swung a thick leg and knocked the gun out of his hand. It skidded across the gore-streaked floor and came to rest in the corner. It may as well have been on the other side of the world.

His adversary was deceptively quick for a big man, but Dylan had a plan. He thrust out both his feet as hard as he could, grunting with satisfaction when his boots connected with the attacker's knees and sent him reeling.

Without getting up, Dylan reached inside his right boot and drew the Double Derringer he kept there for emergencies. Without hesitation, he levelled the gun at the big German, who had composed himself enough to come forward again, and pulled both triggers.

Even in the confined space, the miniature firearm gave off more of a pop than a roar. Dylan was pretty sure both slugs hit home. With the target just feet away he couldn't miss. But the reduced caliber meant they had little stopping power. What they did do was make the big German brute pause. He winced and looked down at his chest and belly, as if to check whether he really had been hit. His once-flawless white apron was now splattered with crimson, but Dylan didn't know how much of it was the German's, how much was Charlie's, and how much was his own.

He needed to finish the job. But there was no time to reload, and the German stood between him and his Peacemaker. What's more, he looked pissed. Striding forward, he clamped his meaty hands around Dylan's throat and lifted him off the floor.

Dylan could feel his windpipe being crushed, and fought off waves of panic as darkness threatened to engulf him. He kicked and lashed out, but he couldn't find any purchase and his energy was quickly draining away.

Then, the mustachioed man let out a scream of rage and hurled Dylan across the room. His back collided with the wall, knocking the breath out of him and sending shooting pains through his ribs.

Head still spinning, Dylan looked up to see the German advancing on him once more. From his position on the blood-soaked floor, his attacker looked even larger than he did when Dylan was standing. Monstrous, even, Like some kind of demented carnival strongman. The look of fury in his eyes told Dylan he was done playing.

Just then, something on the edge of his vision caught his eye. It glittered like treasure. He instinctively reached for it, praying it was his Colt.

It wasn't.

But when the fingers of his right hand closed around the handle of the meat cleaver, he realized it was the next best thing.

He swung the tool in an arc just above knee height, relishing the sense of triumph when the cold steel buried itself deep in the flesh of the big German's thigh.

The scream reverberated around the tiny room, and only increased in volume when Dylan wiggled the cleaver from side to side to create enough give to pull it out.

For a moment the German hopped on his good leg, his face contorted into a mask of pain. Then he abruptly slumped to the floor, reaching for his wounded limb as if his palms held the ability to heal.

The balance of power had now shifted, and Dylan knew he had to make it count. He scrambled to his knees, slipping and sliding in puddles of blood, took aim, and brought the meat cleaver down as hard as he could. The German saw the blow coming and tried to roll out of the way.

He was only partially successful.

The lethally sharpened blade sheared off the crown of his head, including his closely cropped hair, and cracked his skull to reveal the gray brain tissue beneath. A look of confusion fell over him, a look which transformed into one of absolute terror when he saw the cleaver descending for the last time.

Dylan got shakily to his feet, still trying to wrap his head around what had just happened. Hunched over, he carefully prodded at his ribcage. Everything seemed intact, which was a bonus. Leaving the cleaver embedded in the big German's face, he stooped to retrieve his Colt, wiped the blood off it on the dead man's apron, and checked on Charlie Robbins. He was dead, which was probably for the best.

It was time to go before some angry townsfolk turned up and demanded to know why he had killed their famed sausage maker.

Wiping his face on his shirt sleeve, Dylan stepped over the bodies and out into the store. There, he stopped in his tracks. Blocking the exit was the huge German man with the white apron he had just killed.

VI

- -

DYLAN FELT LIKE SOMEONE had kicked him in the belly. How could this be possible?

"I just killed you!" he roared.

Glancing behind him, he saw the body of the big German sprawled on the floor of the storeroom, the meat cleaver still lodged in his face.

Then, Dylan understood.

"Brothers. There are two of you."

"I was upstairs," the other man replied in an accent slightly less polished than his dead brother's leading Dylan to conclude that, shockingly, the dead brother must have been the sociable one. "Heard noise and come see."

"Too late to help your brother," Dylan interjected.

"That's too bad," the German replied candidly. "There used to be three of us rather than just the two, but the winter of '73 was tough. Helmut sustained us for weeks."

"Sustained you?" "Right." "You...ate your own brother?"

"Would you prefer we ate someone else's?" the man asked. "Helmut lost the coin toss. One in three chance. Decent odds. It could have been me, or Heinrich, who I see you've already met. Usually, we mince up strangers passing through Wagnerville. Most are outlaws and vagabonds not missed by many.The sausage shop is a family tradition brought over from Bavaria in 1867. That was a difficult period in our history, with Otto von Bismarck fighting wars with everyone both internal and external. Our family saw the opportunity of a new life and took it. We knew our sausages would be a success here in the land of the free. Nobody can resist them. It's the special ingredient."

"Which is what?"

"I think you've already discovered our secret."

"H-human flesh?" Dylan stammered. "People meat?"

"Give the man a prize! They aren't conscious most of the time. We cut the meat off in strips, tenderize it, put it through the mincer and mix it with pork and offal. Then we cook it up with fat and some salt and spices."

"That's disgusting," Dylan said.

"Not what you said earlier. 'Best thing you ever ate,' I think were your words."

"That was before..." Dylan stopped mid-sentence. "You mean the sausage I ate..."

"Contained bits of the man in there," the huge German said with a smug smile. "There's a certain skill to it. We take the legs first so they can't run away. Then the arms. We try to control the bleeding 'cause if they die too soon the meat goes bad."

Dylan could contain himself no longer. He bowed his head and vomited yellow fluid on the floor and down the front of his shirt. He looked down at the half-digested lumps of chewed-up meat and thought about Charlie Robbins.

"You made me eat my friend!"

"Friend? We heard you talking. Seems he stole your horse and left you to die."

"Okay," Dylan admitted. "Maybe we weren't that close. I might even have wanted to hurt him at one point. But I didn't want the kid made into sausages and fed to me."

"Well, I guess that's just too bad," the man said sardonically.

He wasn't going to let Dylan walk out of here. Dylan didn't know how much the rest of the town knew about the goings-on here at the sausage shop, but that much was clear. For his part, Dylan didn't want to let this monster live another moment. He wanted revenge not just for Charlie Robbins, thieving toad as he was, but also for all the other people these crazed brothers had killed over the years and would in the future.

Dylan was quick on the draw. That part was easy. The mistake most people made was taking too long to aim. Knowing they might only have time to fire once, they heaped pressure on themselves. You had to go by instinct, feel the target, and be confident shooting from the hip. Above all, you had to trust yourself.

The time for talk was over.

Dylan drew and fired three shots in quick succession, filling the seated area of the sausage shop with acrid grey smoke.

But the man no longer occupied the space he did just a split second before.

Shit.

Now Dylan had to move. He took a couple steps to one side and dropped to one knee to present a smaller target.

And it was just as well he did.

There was a deafening *BOOM* and the wall behind Dylan was suddenly peppered with holes. They must have kept a shotgun behind the counter.

Dylan couldn't see where the second brother was. He squeezed off another two rounds, more to buy himself some time than in any hope of hitting the target, and moved position again.

Then, through the drifting clouds of smoke, he spotted the barrel of a shotgun emerge from behind the wall of a booth, and with it half a face.

That was enough.

Dylan took careful aim and emptied the last chamber of his six-shooter. The face disappeared from view and the shotgun clattered to the floor.

Dylan opened the barrel of his Peacemaker, emptied the spent cartridges onto the floor, and quickly reloaded. Then he cautiously approached the booth, expecting the crazed German cannibal sausage maker to leap out at him any second.

It didn't happen.

The second brother was lying on his back over a table, shot clean through the right eye. The bullet had exited through the back of his head, decorating the inside of the booth with his brains. Whoever was cleaning this mess up had one hell of a job on their hands.

All the noise would have alerted the townsfolk, and whether they knew what was in the sausages or not, they would be coming. By the letter of the law, Dylan had just committed a double murder.

He ran out of the sausage shop, mounted Skydance, and rode out of Wagnerville without looking back.

VII

P HEW. THE MEMORY ALONE made his skin crawl. That was the thing about Christmas. It brought everything back. Both good and bad.

How many strangers had ended up being slathered in sauerkraut and mustard and served to unwitting customers in those warm bread rolls in Wagnerville? Dozens? Hundreds?

As he and Skydance pushed on through the chill, huge, fluffy snowflakes began falling all around them. Dylan was reminded for the first time in a long time that though there was endless wickedness, villainy and depravity in the world, there were also brief moments of extreme beauty which made everything worthwhile. That was why we kept going. Those bright spots in the darkness.

He plucked out a carrot, an apple, and a sugar cube he had been keeping in his coat pocket, leaned forward, and fed them to Skydance, giving the horse time between offerings to savour the exquisite flavours.

"Merry Christmas, boy."

When he looked up, he saw lights flickering in the distance. There was a town coming up. Every new town represented a new beginning. There would probably be lots of fun and merriment, whiskey and women. He might be able to get that soft bed, bath, and hot meal he had been dreaming of.

He just hoped sausages weren't on the menu.

BUY AND SAVE

$1.00 OFF

WHEN YOU PURCHASE C.M. SAUNDER'S

NOVELLA, *SILENT MINE* AT

UNDERTAKERBOOKS.COM

eBook or paperback

CODE: DECKER

Silent Mine

Dylan Decker is a drifter trying to stay alive in the Californian badlands, a place awash with vagabonds, bandits, tribes of hostile natives, and worse. In the autumn of 1879 he finds himself in a dying frontier town by the name Hope's Creek on the trail of a missing gold prospector. His last known location was Silent Mine, a place shrouded in myth and enshrined in folklore. The locals say it contains riches beyond your wildest imagination, but it comes at a heavy cost. Because if you enter Silent Mine, you might never make it back out.

Blood Lake

Riding east through the Rockies after his adventure at *Silent Mine,* Dylan Decker gets tangled up with a grizzly bear, and finds himself neck-deep in another dangerous situation.
The town of Dudsville has been plagued by the Winged Terror for longer

than most folks there can remember. Dylan is tempted to keep riding, but he feels obliged to the townspeople who showed him such kindness in the aftermath of the grizzly fight. So when the Winged Terror drops in, he agrees to join a small posse in pursuit of the beast.

But is the posse hunting the Winged Terror, or is the Winged Terror hunting them?

A battle rages through the foothills of the Rockies as Dylan and his friends match wits with a beast unlike anything he's faced before. Can they bring down the Winged Terror, or will the monster slip away to terrorize another generation?

About the Author

Chris Saunders, who writes fiction as C.M. Saunders, is a freelance journalist and editor from South Wales. His work has appeared in hundreds of magazines, ezines, journals and anthologies worldwide including Fortean Times, Writer's Weekly, Writer's Digest, the Literary Hatchet, ParABnormal, Fantastic Horror, Haunted MTL, Feverish Fiction and Crimson Streets. His books have been both traditionally and independently published, his latest release being Silent Mine: A Dylan Decker Mystery on Undertaker Books.

Keep up to date by visiting his website:
https://cmsaunders.wordpress.com/

Or following his socials:
@CMSaunders01
https://www.facebook.com/CMSaunders01/